This igloo book belongs to:

....

Published in 2013
by Igloo Books Ltd
Cottage Farm
Sywell
NN6 0BJ
www.igloobooks.com

FIR003 1013
8 10 12 11 9 7
ISBN: 978-0-85780-427-3

Printed and manufactured in China

Be Brave, Little Penguin

igloobooks

Little Penguin looks just like all the other penguins.

He has a little orange beak. He has two tiny wings.

He has a soft white tummy.

But Little Penguin is not like all the other penguins.

He doesn't like diving under the blue waves.
He doesn't like splashing in the sparkling ocean.

Little Penguin is
scared of the water.

Everyone loves playing in the snow.
Little Penguin likes the ice helter skelter best.

He slides around...

... and around...

... and around!

"This is so much fun!"
giggles Little Penguin.

The other penguins dive into the water.
"Come with us, Little Penguin!" they call.
But Little Penguin is too scared.

Everyone loves sliding on the ice.

...and spin...

...and skid.

Little Penguin goes fastest of all.

But then...

"HELP!"

...

He wibbles and wobbles on the very edge.

"I nearly fell in!" he gasps.
And his little wings tremble.

"Poor Little Penguin," says Little Seal Cub.
"Don't worry, I'll play with you." Little Penguin and
Little Seal Cub race and chase each other.

They go around the icy glaciers.
And through the powdery snow.

Then... whoops! Little Penguin skids on the ice.
"HELP!" cries Little Penguin.

SWOOSH!

He slides down the snow bank!

Little Penguin is in the water!

At first, he is scared.
But then he kicks his legs... he flaps his little wings...
... and **whoosh!** Suddenly he's swimming!

"This isn't scary!" says Little Penguin. "This is fun!"

Little Penguin plops back onto the ice.

"That was great!" he laughs.

"Do you want to do it again?" asks Little Seal Cub.

"Yes please!" says Little Penguin.

Then, he sees Little Polar Bear standing on the ice.

"Come and play with us," calls Little Penguin.
"I'm not sure," whispers Little Polar Bear.
"The water is a bit scary."

Little Penguin gives a great, big smile.
"I know exactly how you feel," he says.
"I used to be scared, too."

WHEEEEEEE!

Little Penguin and Little Polar Bear slide and splash into the water.

Little Penguin and his friends had lots of fun playing in the sea. "I'll never be scared of the water again," said Little Penguin. And he never was.

"Goodbye, see you soon!"